THE FIRST DAY SPEECH

STORY BY **ISABELLE HADALA**

ILLUSTRATED BY **JOSÉ PARDO**

Wild Onion Press
BOOKS STARRING KIDS WITH
PHYSICAL DIFFERENCES

Book Design by Walton Dale   www. designwellstudio.com

First edition

ISBN 978-1-4675-2444-5, Library of Congress Control Number 2012936172

Printed in the United States using environmentally friendly materials

A portion of the proceeds of this book will be donated to Hands to Love Congenital Hand Camp.

Wild Onion Press

BOOKS STARRING KIDS WITH
PHYSICAL DIFFERENCES

352-213-5740   www.wildonionpress.com

THE FIRST DAY SPEECH

STORY BY **ISABELLE HADALA**

ILLUSTRATED BY **JOSÉ PARDO**

Three more days until school starts.

Nathan is so excited, he runs around the house willy-nilly, accidentally bumping into things. Sometimes he hops like a frog with nowhere to go—up and down, up and down.

Then he flops down in exhaustion.

Finally, Nathan is old enough to go to school! He will go off each morning with all the other kids in his neighborhood.

But what will the first day of school be like?

How will he feel being away from home all day?

At night, Nathan tosses and turns in his bed. His older brother Eric seems to be sleeping just fine. Well, not quite just fine. Eric begins wiggling and turning. So Nathan calls out from under his covers, "Are you thinking about the first day of school?"

"Naw," Eric calls back. "I just need a drink of water."

But when Eric comes back with a glass of water, he says, "I just don't know how many of my friends will be in my class this year. Last year there was Tommy and Chad and Will and. . . But Tommy moved. And Chad is going to a different school. And I haven't talked to Will all summer. I'll probably have to make all new friends this year."

"I don't know anybody," says Nathan from under his covers. "Who will be my friend?"

"Oh, Nathan," says Eric with a sigh, "don't sweat it. You'll be fine. Surely somebody will be your friend."

Then Eric rolls over and goes to sleep.

But Nathan isn't so sure that he'll be fine on that first day of school. He doesn't like to meet new people. He doesn't like to be anywhere for very long without his mother or his father or his brother.

What will it be like in that big school on 8th Street? he wonders.

Each year Nathan has visited Eric's classroom. He has gone to see Eric's programs in the big auditorium. But what will it be like for HIM?

Would big boys pick on him?
Would girls tease him?
Would his teacher be nice?

The week before, when the school had an open house, Nathan met Ms. Jenkins, his teacher. "But it's easy to be nice for a little while," he thought. "Maybe she won't be so nice all the other days."

Would anyone play with him on the playground?
Would anyone sit by him at lunch?
And what about his special worry?
Would kids make fun of him?

The next day Nathan shows Eric what he plans to wear on that first day. "Maybe I'll go like this," he says and steps out of the closet in his bank robber outfit.

"I don't think so," says Eric.

"Then what about this?" Nathan puts on a Halloween mask.

"Or I could be a pirate with a beard all over my face.
Or an astronaut with a space helmet, like this."

"No, Nathan. Sorry, buddy. You can't be any of those.
You have to go as nobody but yourself. You have to be you."

That night, Nathan barely sleeps at all.

The next morning at breakfast, Nathan tells his mother, "I've decided something—something about the first day of school."

"Oh, yes?" His mother turns to look at him. "And what might that be? What are you thinking, Nathan?"

"I want to give a speech."
"A speech?" his mother asks, startled.

Nathan squares his shoulders and stands up tall. "Yes, a short speech but a good one. I want to stand up in front of everyone and talk about myself." He then swells out his chest with determination.

His mother looks at him tenderly. Then she nods. "I see.
Well, okay then. But first we must ask your teacher. I don't know that Ms. Jenkins has ever had a request such as this. I think I know what you want to say, though." She smiles. "Last year in preschool, a lot of kids asked you questions. This year, you want to answer their questions before they even ask?"

Nathan nods.

"All right, then," his mother says. "I'll call Ms. Jenkins this afternoon. I'll explain all this."

Nathan smiles and rushes outside to ride skateboards with Eric.

Near suppertime, Nathan's mother comes to flag him down as Nathan whizzes past her. "Ms. Jenkins said, okay. She said she'd never had a student give a speech on the first day of school, but she agreed to it. She said you could give your speech tomorrow morning very first thing."

That night, Nathan falls asleep thinking, "After tomorrow, I'll be a school kid. I'm one of the big guys now. I have to get up early and get ready, just like Eric, and like my mom and dad do for work. School is my work now. And tomorrow I will give my speech."

When the morning light streams through the window, Nathan springs out of bed. He puts on his new school clothes and goes to eat his breakfast. Eric dawdles along like an old fourth-grade sleepyhead.

"I'll drive you to school and stay until you get settled," Nathan's mother says. "No, that's okay," Nathan tells her. "I want to do this by myself."

But really, he's not so sure. His stomach flutters as if a jar of butterflies has been set loose. But bravely, he walks to the bus stop with Eric. His father calls as he drives by on his way to work, "You will be fine, Nathan. And Eric, don't forget Saturday—we have a ballgame."

Nathan smiles, and Eric calls, "Sure thing!"

Then Nathan climbs on the bus and waves confidently back to his mother.

"Don't worry, my little buddy," she calls to him. "You're the king of the five-year-olds in this house, and you'll be the king of lots of things in other places too."

"I know, I know, I know," Nathan calls back. "But golly!" he thinks, "it can be embarrassing to have your mother calling after you with all the other kids around."

At school, Eric walks Nathan to his new classroom. Outside the door, Eric touches Nathan on his shoulder and says, "Don't worry, Bro. I'm just down the hall if you need me."

Then, as Eric walks off, he looks back and teasingly says, "But don't call me unless you get stuck in a Xerox machine or something really drastic like that. Don't bother me if it's something stupid."

But as he says it, he smiles.

Nathan goes to a seat in the back of his new classroom. As all the other kids walk in, they stop and stare at him.

Nathan puts his head in his hands and looks down.

"Good morning," Ms. Jenkins says. She looks out over her new class. "This is such an important day." She smiles while looking at each one of her students. "And I am so lucky to have all of you in my class. We're going to have such a good time every day, all year long! Now, one of your classmates wants to start off the year by making a speech. Yes, a speech." She looks at Nathan and waves him forward.

Nathan walks to the front of the room and stands in front of Ms. Jenkins' desk. Then he turns around and knows that he can't say what he really wants to say: *Get a good look at me and get over it.* That would sound too harsh. It would also be rude.

He has to tell the truth in a way that will make them all understand. They have to learn not to make fun of him.

What bothers him more than people staring are the one-hundred questions they often ask, such as, "Does it hurt?" "Can I catch it?" "Will my face get split and messed up too?" "Was it a shark or a lawn mower that did that to you?" "Can you see okay?" and "If you fall down, will you break?"

"Hello, my name is Nathan," he begins. His knees shake, and he feels a little dizzy. "I know it's easy to see that I look different. And I know you are wondering what happened to me. I can tell you quite simply, my face is not contagious. If you touch my cheek, it will not hurt. I can eat and laugh and tell jokes just like you. I was born this way, and it is not 'catching.'"

The classroom is so quiet that Nathan can tell that everyone is listening closely. So he goes on with the next part of his speech. "An operation put me together the best it could. And believe me, I look a whole lot better now than when I came into the world!" At that, he laughs, and some in the class laugh with him. "That's also why I talk a little funny."

"Yeah," a boy calls out. "You sound like you have a cold!"

A girl in the back stands up. "You sound like my sister when her nose gets stopped up with allergies," she says.

"Yeah," another girl blurts out, waving her arm. "My grandfather got a big knot on his cheek and he had to have it cut off. It was a skin cancer caused by the sun. And he has a scar now that goes all down his face like this." She runs her finger down her own cheek. "And for a whole year he couldn't eat apples. He had to eat stuff mashed up in a blender."

A boy right in front of Nathan stands up." Look here!" He says, "I have a funny finger. I got it stuck in a wire fence when I was a baby. I don't remember it. But my mother says I broke it. I even broke the wire! And my finger's grown crooked ever since. Want to see it up close?"

Ms. Jenkins interrupts. "Thank you, Sam. We'll take a look later. Let's let Nathan finish his speech right now."

"But look at this!" another big boy says, jumping up. He tilts his head back. "I got a rock stuck up in my nose when I was three years old, and I've always thought it made my nose have a bulge. Can you see this here?"

"All right, class, all right," Ms. Jenkins says. "Let's sit in a circle now.
I want to ask you something."

She walks next to Nathan, gently puts her hand on his shoulder and asks,
"Who will be Nathan's friend today?
Who will play with him at recess?
Who will walk with him to the lunch room?
Who will be his reading partner at reading time?"

Hands shoot up. And the voices calling out are many and loud. The chorus of "Me, Me. I will, I will" sounds like excited birds chattering in a forest of trees.

Some even sing out,
"I'll be his friend for more than today,"
"I'll be his friend all week,"
"I'll be his friend all year,"
"I'll be his friend for life!"

Nathan laughs. He walks over and sits down in the circle with all his new friends.

He feels his special worry lifting. He feels it falling away like a rock into a river and being swept away.

Oh yes, his speech was a hit. Everyone now sees that there is no reason to make fun of him or of anyone. They are all different in their different ways.

He hadn't even had to say the last part of his speech!— the part where he'd planned to say, "Always, I see myself as a natural wonder. And I hope you will think of me that way too."

For already, it was clear—the class saw him in an even better way than he'd hoped.

They saw him as Nathan, a new friend.

NATHAN

Nathan is a fictional character. He has a facial cleft, a condition that results from one side of a child's face failing to develop normally in the womb. No one knows exactly what causes a facial cleft, but surgery greatly improves the condition, so that most children like Nathan have only small, noticeable differences.

Yet, any difference can be worrisome to a child, especially when meeting new people. Indeed, most children are apprehensive about that first day of school when so much is unknown.

Nathan represents all children, especially those who have a special fear of being accepted just as they are.

ISABELLE HADALA

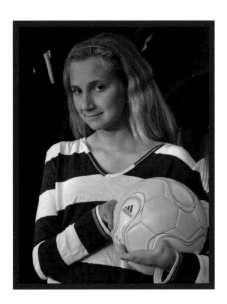

When Isabelle Hadala was six years old and about to enter first grade, she told her mother that she wanted to give a speech on the first day of school. In preschool, her classmates had asked so many questions about her hands and feet that she now wanted to simply address such curiosity all at once.

"Izzy" was born with Ectodermal Dysplasia, a condition that halted the development of most of her fingers, teeth and toes. Her unusual request led to an annual first-day-of-school speech through which Izzy makes each child feel welcome by inspiring understanding and igniting compassion.

In fifth grade, Izzy won a Disney Dreamer and Doer award by writing an essay in which she said, "Even though I have this condition, I know that it is only a part of me and not who I am entirely. My biggest goal in life is to teach children that kids who look different are the same as everyone else."

Today Izzy is a middleschooler in Orlando, Florida, a ferocious soccer player and an ambassador for children with physical differences. When she was in elementary school, she produced her school's daily news program with the same spunk and confidence with which she delivered her first day speech.

In this picture book, Izzy's speech on her first day of first grade has now become Nathan's story. As Nathan's speech clearly shows, we are all alike in our own different ways; and furthermore, Izzy and Nathan are major cool.

JOSÉ PARDO

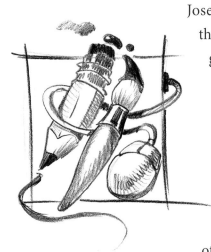

Jose Pardo was born in Havana, Cuba, and came to the United States with his family as a young boy. He graduated with a Bachelor's Degree in Fine Arts from New Jersey City University, after which he moved to Orlando, Florida, and developed his skills in digital illustration. For seven years, he worked at Disney designing and illustrating art for merchandise for the theme parks, worldwide— including the grand opening artwork for Hong Kong Disneyland. Currently, he is a graphic artist in the merchandising department of Universal Studios Florida. He is an avid soccer player and fan, fitting in his love of sports with his busy schedule. For Nathan's first day speech, he sketched the illustrations in pencil, then applied color digitally, for although he was traditionally trained, he now embraces the new technology that has so quickly changed the world of graphic arts.